EDEN *miniatures*

EDEN *miniatures*

# INSOMNIA

*Optimist*

Insomnia

First Edition

*Insomnia* was first published as part of *EDEN by FREI*
*– a concept narrative in the here & now about the where,*
*the wherefore and forever* at *EDENbyFREI.net*



ISBN: 978-1-64370-449-4

Optimist Books by Optimist Creations

optimistcreations.com

Insomnia

# {Connexum}

not the essay, just the idea
not the notion that everything is
connected, that is not new
and not the question
how connected is everything
but the question
how
if everything is connected
is everything connected

if things are connected
there must be something that connects
them

and for many things that are connected
we know what that is
we can see it, measure it, build it, make it
we can name it:
the axles the shafts

the electric current the
data the code and the signal

but what about things that are connected
and we
don't know what it is that connects them
what about
quantum entanglement
for example, albert einstein's
*spukhafte fernwirkung*
what about that?

there is no doubt that things are connected
of which
we don't know how this is
and
if things are connected
there has to be some thing that connects
them
even if that is
a thing we have not detected

a thing we have not yet detected and so not
yet given a name to
a thing we have not yet detected but may
yet find
we can find

that would give us
three things in principle:
energy
information
and the third thing
the thing that connects things
for which we don't yet have a name
but we have
maybe
names
for manifestations of it
the strong and weak nuclear forces
the electromagnetic force and the force of
gravity

what if these forces are to the third thing as

light sound heat motion are to the first
(energy)
and as
data code and semantic content are to the
second (information)
what if that third thing is a thing in itself
that exists and that is
as yet only
partly
understood

as humans we like sets of threes
trios, triumvirates, trinities
they give us a deeper reality

at first glance we seem to be living in twos
in the binaries of
male/female
plus/minus
hot/cold
dark/light
day/night

yes/no
1/0

but it only takes one thought to know
that
neat and simple as this looks and sounds
it is patently not our
reality

our reality
here too
needs a third component each time:

male/trans/female
plus/neutral/minus
hot/tepid/cold
dark/twilight/light
yes/maybe/no
1/anything in between/0

even yin and yang are not a duality

but a symbolic expression of the way
apparent opposites complement each other
as part of
the same

and this
is when it gets really interesting, when
dualities are not augmented by that which
is in between
but are understood as the whole:

yin/same/yang

for which the quantum equivalent then
could be
on/on-and-off-at-the-same-time/off

what if
we've always known this to be the case
and have expressed it in many ways
the elements of
the same the other and the essence

in plato's *timaeus*
the father the son and the holy spirit
*anicca, dukkha, anattā:*
impermanence
suffering
non-self

what if that third thing
the essence, the holy spirit, the non-self
is
in principle
the thing that connects
everything

the third thing
the thing for which we don't yet have a
name but that exists and that
we most likely
will find and be able to identify, a

connexum?

{The Fire Breather}

Though he be strong, he is not fierce;
though he be powerful, he is not violent.
Although he be dependable, righteous he
can't be; though he be wise, he is not heard.
He is a Fire Breather: his word burns like a
torch; like Elijah's does it purify – but can
it ever be understood? By whom?

He casts a curious figure in the wilderness,
as he stands by the shore, by the riverbank,
on the mountain, on the traffic island in
the city; in the square; shadowless, peerless,
ageless. The inner beauty of his mind
obscured and masked by the dust on his
brow and the mud round his ankles. His
hair all a-tangle, his white beard streaked
now only with the occasional charcoal,
with a strand of dark blond here, or there

ginger. His scent is not sweet, nor is he a
joy to behold, at first glance.

At second glance the wrinkles around
his eyes show as laugh lines, and they are
merry with wisdom. At third glance the
light in his eyes shines bright as a flame:
the oxygen of an insight beyond.

Through meditation and study and
practice he has mastered the art of putting
his mind above matter, and so he has learnt
to walk on water, but he can only do so
when nobody watches because he knows
that if anyone were to see him, they would
turn him into a miracle worker, a prophet,
a freak. A messiah. A wonder of no more
worth than that it defies the simple laws of
contemporarily understood physics.

He will not have it. He will not be
entertainment. He will not speak of his

understanding, nor will he surmise his
premonitions other than to those who are
able and willing to pause. And stay silent,
but for a while. Ere they ask questions.
Those who are capable of phrasing these
questions from a hunger for knowledge,
a desire to learn. They are not many. The
shouting, the screaming, the screeching,
the demands for explanations, the sarcastic
tones and the jibes, the heckling, the
laughter, the desire—the instinct—for
tearing him down, the lust for his failure,
for his destruction, for him to be hung
drawn and quartered, for his undoing, are
great.

He knows this, and he inwardly smiles. He
has the capacity in his heart to forgive. He
is magnanimous in his disposition towards
those who hate him, who wish him
silenced, who relish him misunderstood.
Because he knows: one day something or

someone will catch fire from his word and the fire will spread and will cause a great conflagration from which the lands will emerge purged and fertile for new thought to grow.

That is not his aim nor his goal nor his intention, that is just his purpose. His purpose is to quietly whisper into the din of the crowd that will not heed him, and plant the seeds he was given to sow. Until one takes hold. Until from just one or just two or just three or four, and then four or five more, some thing starts to grow.

He doesn't even know what that could be. He has no certainty that it will not be dangerous, poisonous even, or be made such by others who will take what they find and turn it upside down, inside out; who pervert him and his gentle teachings into dogma and strife. He cannot prevent this from happening, if it must. He can only be true to his purpose, his purpose being his word.

Fear not the Fire Breather, but neither dismiss or ignore him. And doubt not the might of the Word.

now the problem of the giraffe taking a
shower is a very serious one which has
never really been solved. it is also very
much doubtful whether it ever will be
solved, since it is such a vexed and great
one.

the giraffe taking a shower has the great
problem that the water running down his
beautiful long ears, down his beautiful long
neck, over his delightful belly, and down
his beautiful long legs, reaches his beautiful
long toes when it is not likely to be quite
as warm any more as it was when it rinsed
over those beautiful long ears. in fact is is
very likely to be rather cold.

thus the giraffe taking a shower finds
himself confronted with the everlasting

conundrum of an undisintangleable
dilemma.

this sounds unlikely, i know, that is we all
know, you and i know it sounds remarkably
unlikely, but it is nevertheless very true:
should he, the giraffe taking a shower, risk
burning the tips of his beautiful ears, or
perchance freeze to the bone his beautiful
toes.

if he sets the water temperature too high,
he will invariably burn the tips of his
beautiful ears, or at the very least get very
hot in his head, which is almost equally
uncomfortable; does he, however, try
to avoid this by tuning the water a little
colder, he will of course not burn his ears,
but by the time the water will have run
down all of his beautiful long neck, his
delightful belly will already shiver a little,
and when the water finally reaches his

beautiful long toes it will be plain cold, and
he will awfully chill his sensitive foot ends.

so this, as most easily can be understood, is
the problem of the giraffe taking a shower.
what is he supposed to do: should he drop
the idea of having a shower altogether
and instead take the occasional bath?
that, of course, might seem like a sensible
alternative. but how complicated a thing
to do. for a giraffe. no-one could expect
him to just simply fold his neck when he
wants to wash it, and how can he reach his
beautiful ears when his beautiful long legs
still are not half as long as his beautiful
neck.

oh i can tell you, a giraffe has no easy life
to live. his problems are many, and none of
them is a small one, let alone short. he or
she, the giraffe taking a shower, is a poor
creature indeed, just like you and like me...

Insomnia

I never lost much sleep over losing sleep.
Doing so seemed, well, counterintuitive.
Illogical. Self-defeating.

Those friends—one or two—who
complained of restless nights, of tossing
and turning, of simply not switching off,
baffled me: why not just get up, if you can't
sleep, and do some work, I would wonder.
Or if you don't do the kind of work you
can pursue in the small hours of the night
or the morning, why not, maybe, read?
Or watch a film? Watch a documentary
for example, or a history programme?
Phone a friend in New Zealand, or in
Australia: there's bound to be one you've
mostly forgotten about, because they never
comment on social media. They're actually
there: just call them up out of the blue and

say: 'hey! How is it all hanging with you?'
It will be a lovely surprise.

'Oh, but then I'll be tired in the morning,'
my sleepless friends would say. But you'll
be tired in the morning anyway, I'd
think and say: 'I see. That's inconvenient,
certainly.' I didn't really see. Though I
realised it would be inconvenient to be
tired in the morning. Then again they were
tired in the morning anyway, because they
couldn't sleep, so why not be tired having
done something useful, or interesting?

A very good friend of mine who often
found it difficult to sleep told me she
worried a great deal about it, because it
made her feel neurotic. I half bethought
me there was perhaps a seed of self-
knowledge contained in this sensation. I
didn't think it friendly to say so, so I said,
'I'm so sorry to hear that.' She would go

to bed at nine thirty, ten at the latest, and
then lie awake. She used to use earplugs
and a sleep mask and close the heavy
curtains of her bedroom. And not sleep.
'You never have that problem?' I never had
that problem.

I can sleep in any kind of setting, light
or dark; I have a high background noise
threshold (I mostly just zone out of it), I
sleep any time, day or night; my window,
except during coldest winter, is always
ajar, my blinds don't darken the room,
they just afford a bit of privacy; I usually
go to bed about three, three thirty in the
morning (sometimes, if it's been a heavy
day or an early start, or an early start is
impending, an hour or so earlier), I sleep
until ten, maybe nine-thirty; I don't set an
alarm unless I absolutely have to: my body
appears to require seven hours of sleep
now, almost exactly, to wake up, slowly and

a little reluctantly, always, but essentially to
fully functioning order restored. So long as
I'm warm enough, I am fine. I don't even
mind my lover snoring. I simply clamp
onto him and fall in with his breathing, no
problem.

The problem started when Edgar, my
most sensible friend, told me he couldn't
sleep. 'Why not?' I asked him. He said
he didn't know, he just couldn't. It was
annoying. Beyond annoying, it was tiring:
he's a university lecturer, he needs to be
awake during the day, to do his thinking,
his preparing of lectures, his reading,
and his lecturing. Being tired is not just
inconvenient for him, it's debilitating.
Suddenly that made sense. And now I
was worried. If Edgar, my least neurotic
and quite possibly most intelligent friend,
suddenly, out of the blue, simply can't
sleep, and for no particular reason, but

to the point where it interferes with his operability, then who is safe from this menace? I decided, uncharacteristically, to probe further:

'Has anything happened to make you lose sleep over it?'

'Not really, no.'

'Your relationship is going well.'

'Splendid. Except we sleep in separate rooms at the moment, because I can't sleep. And I snore.'

'Aw. – Ah well, many couples sleep in separate rooms.'

'They do.'

'Your children are healthy?'

'They're excellent, thanks.'

'Your daughter-in-law has calmed down a bit.'

'A bit. It'll take her a while, I suppose.'

'I suppose. – University not undergoing too many changes, no upheavals?'

'Just the bureaucracy, it's creeping in, it's taking over. It's a nightmare.'

'Ah! There you go! You are worried about the bureaucrats taking over!'

'No I don't worry about them, I've got tenure. They just annoy me, they have no imagination.'

'Of course not, they're bureaucrats. How about… how about… food? You eat well, don't you?'

This is an unnecessary question: Edgar eats exquisitely: he is one of the best chefs I know.

'There really is no obvious reason,' he says, a tone of resignation in his voice.

That worries me: if Edgar, of all people, quite possibly the most up-for-it, can-do person I know, is sounding resigned over being unable to sleep, then who can fight this disease. *Disease!*

'How is your health?'

'My health is all right, thanks, how is yours?'

'Mine is just dandy, thanks. Do you take any exercise?' I've recently latched on to the need to take exercise, it's an age thing; has Edgar?

'Of course not.'

'Maybe that's the cause of your inability to sleep.'

'I have never taken any exercise in my life, I burn all my calories in my brain.' This is probably true. The brain uses a lot of energy, and Edgar is one of the most avid thinkers I know; but thinking doesn't aid circulation.

'You maybe should go for a walk now and then.'

'I go for short walks all the time.'

'Maybe you should go for a long walk, every day.'

'You do that, don't you?'

'I do. And I sleep like a baby.'

'What, wake up every few hours and scream your head off, until somebody rocks you and gives you some oral gratification.'

'I walked right into that, didn't I.' That's why I like Edgar, he doesn't take any nonsense from me, or from anyone. And he's brought up a whole brood of children, he knows what he's talking about.

'Have you thought about therapy?' (Of course he hasn't.)

'Of course not.'

'Then I don't know what I can recommend. Read, maybe. *Hitchhiker's Guide to the Galaxy*. People rave about it. I tried reading it five times, I fell asleep every time. It's like a switch: I get to about page three, four, maximum five, then I'm out. Just like that.'

'I've read it. It was entertaining.'

'Maybe try reading it again… – or: maybe try reading about something you're really not interested in, at all.'

'Like what?'

'Like the Spanish Civil War.'

'The Spanish Civil War?'

'Yes: are you interested in the Spanish Civil War?'

'I have never given it a moment's thought.'

'Try that.'

I meet Edgar for coffee about two weeks later, as we are both in town. (We are not that often both in town at the same time, we lead busy, cosmopolitan lifestyles that involve being out of and in other cities and towns respectively all the time.)

'How is it going?

'Fine thanks. Just very tired.'

'Still no joy with the sleep?'

'It's getting worse.'

'I'm sorry to hear that.'

'Thanks. You are, of course, to blame.'

'Me?'

'Yes.'

'How come?'

'Well, I started reading about the Spanish Civil War: it's fascinating!'

'Oh, but that's great, isn't it?

'Yes and no: I'm learning about European history, which, frankly, I knew little about, but the books now keep me awake even longer.'

'Ah. Well. That was an unintended consequence. Maybe you have to find something less stimulating to read, and less likely to be of random tangential relevance to you. How about botany?'

'Botany?'

'Yes, you don't have a garden, do you.'

'No.'

'And you don't want one, do you.'

'Absolutely not.'

'Well there you go: why not read about botany, that will send you to sleep.' (If that doesn't send him to sleep, I think, then nothing will. Then again, there are botanists, so who knows...)

It's nearly the end of June and I'm about to go on a lengthy trip, so I forget about the business of sleep for a while as I cruise around Europe in an open top car. This feels both extravagant and romantic. I'm doing it on my own, because I don't at that point have a partner, and I'm enjoying the freedom, the spirit, the air. I sleep in a different *b'n'b* every night, almost, and most of the time on my own. Only on one occasion is the host so flirtatious, so attractive, so sexy that we end up spending the night together. In Bordeaux. I eat well, I drink well, I sleep well.

Edgar and I are having dinner, on my return. He's cooking, the way he usually does, in passing. He has the knack for rustling up something delicious as if it weren't happening, while we're talking. It's fascinating, and a little disconcerting. When I cook (which I only do since recently, thanks to an online service that sends me all the ingredients in a box, together with clear instructions, which I follow to the letter and get annoyed with if they are even remotely vague, which thankfully happens extremely rarely), I have to give it my full concentration. I follow the steps. My cooking is in essence a connecting of dots: it's reading the sheet music and making it work. With some success, I might add. Edgar's cooking is all jazz and improvisation. The steak is particularly juicy on this occasion, and the roasted vegetables with fresh herbs are out of this world!

'You've surpassed yourself, Edgar! This food is amazing!'

'Thanks.'

'The vegetables, they are so tasty!' (I notice I'm discoursing in exclamation marks, all of a sudden! But they're warranted!)

'Thanks.' Edgar is humility personified. 'I grew them during the summer.'

'You what?'

'I grew them, in the garden.'

'You don't have a garden. – Do you?'

'I do: I asked the neighbour down on the ground floor who tended the garden and he said nobody does, it's a crying shame, and so I said: let me.'

'But you know nothing about gardening.'

'Well, I've been reading a lot about botany lately, and it's really quite the most interesting thing. And stimulating.'

'O-oh.'

'I know, it doesn't send me to sleep, of course; it keeps me awake, but hey: we have exquisite vegetables now, and those herbs.'

I fear me I may have to change me my strategy...

Five o'clock in the morning: I lie awake,
worrying about Edgar. Not about Edgar
himself, obviously, Edgar is the last person
I need to worry about: I worry about the
fact that Edgar of all people can't sleep,
and what that means for someone like me,
who normally sleeps without a hint of a
problem, when I thought Edgar was the
kind of person who did so too; does that
mean I have to worry about not being able
to sleep, all of a sudden, just like Edgar?

It's the kind of worry I least appreciate
and am least able to see any sense in: it's
worrying about worrying: it's a meta-worry.
It's a preposterousness, and that is in itself
a worry: I now worry about the fact that I
worry. About worrying.

My lover doesn't notice I'm lying awake
next to him, worrying, he just rasps a
contented snore. He's an uncomplicated
sleeper. Sometimes he has nightmares
that wake him up briefly, but he goes
back to sleep easily and quickly. I think it
might just be my clamping onto him that
occasionally sets off a nightmare in him,
but I don't ask for fear that he'll confirm
that, yes, that's what it is, because I like
snuggling up to him: I spend the whole
night resting my head on his chest, holding
him; he holding me.

I arrange to see Edgar for a drink and he
seems very happy. Tired, but fulfilled. In
the course of our conversation—it's been
a while since we last met, so we have some
catching up to do—I realise he's become
an expert in about a half dozen subjects,
and he does not seem the least bit worried,

about any of them, or about getting enough sleep:

'Oh no,' he laughs: I nap.'

'You nap?'

'Yes.'

'When do you nap?'

'When I'm tired.'

'And then you sleep?'

'No I nap, there's a difference...'

'I realise there's a difference, but then at night, do you sleep?'

'Oh no, at night I lie awake, reading.'

'What are you reading about?'

'At the moment I'm learning Rumantsch.'

'You're learning Rumantsch by reading?'

'I read it at night, and practise it during the day.'

'Rumantsch?'

'Yes.'

'So you speak Rumantsch now?'
'I read it quite well.'

I feel a little tired just listening to Edgar,
as he tells me he has taken to translating a
Rumantsch story into English.
'Aren't you tired?'
'No, I've just had a nap.'
'I mean generally: how much sleep
do you get?'
'It varies: between four and five
hours a day, enough to survive.'
'And you're not tired? You look a
bit tired.'
'Oh that's probably because I've
just woken up from my nap: it takes me a
while...'
'What are you going to do with
your Rumantsch story, once you've
translated it into English?
'I can read it to you.'

'Yes you could: that might actually send me to sleep.'

The experiment is not a success. I am too weirded out by the fact that I have a man twice my size but effectively my age sitting in my living room, reading me a story. Also, the story is quite interesting. When I tell my lover, he suggests I read it to him: he dozes off straight away.

I sit awake, reading the rest of the story that Edgar has translated from Rumantsch into English, about an alp farmer and his three sons, who all become mercenaries, fighting wars for foreign lords in far flung countries, for remuneration. One dies, one is captured and spends a long time being held hostage because his family can't afford the ransom, and one comes back, traumatised, but determined to bring home his brother. He sets off again on what turns into a riveting adventure of selfless bravery, Helvetian heroism and blockheaded stubbornness. He finds and liberates his brother, and his brother is grateful but also sad: he does not want to leave his fellow prisoner of war behind whom he has become close friends with: as close as brothers, closer even. Blood brothers. I think lovers, but the story doesn't spell that out. It was written by a descendant of the older, stronger, rescuing brother in the early part of the 18th century, and they didn't so much go in for the gay theme, at the time. To me it's pretty obvious. My lover is fast asleep, so I can't ask him.

I phone Edgar, sure to find him awake: he answers the phone straight away:

'Of course, it's obvious!'

'Do you think the story would make a good film?'

'Of course it would make a good film!'

'Do you think I should write a treatment?'

'Why not? I'm not going to!'

'Who owns the rights?'

'I don't think anybody does, but I can find out for you!'

Now Edgar is full of exclamation marks, which wearies me, this time of night, but I'm glad that what keeps me awake now is no longer my meta-worry about worrying about being worried about Edgar, but thinking about how to frame this stupendous tale into a good, solid, rustic, heroic love story. Between a Helvetian mercenary and his lover in captivity. Over the next couple of weeks I write the treatment during my night time waking hours and show it to Edgar.

'It's quite good.'

'Quite good.'

'Yes, but you're missing something.'

'What am I missing?'

'You're missing the Rumantschness.'

'The Rumantschness?'

'Yes. You've got the Helvetianness all right, which is not surprising, seeing you're Helvetian yourself, but you're missing the Rumantschness.'

'How do I get the Rumantschness?'

'I don't know: go there, talk to the clan, learn Rumantsch…'

'You want me to learn Rumantsch?'

'I don't want you to learn it, I want you to get the Rumantschness of it: if you want someone to finance this project for you so you can turn it into a film that will be shown at the Locarno Film Festival, and be owned by the people you're talking about at the same time, then you've got to get the Rumantschness of it all.'

I hadn't thought anywhere near as far ahead as that, but of course he is right: this is exactly the kind of film that should be shown at the Locarno Film Festival, preferably on the Piazza Grande, and be both good enough to be able to win a jury award and have enough of a broad appeal—with its Helvetian 17th century prisoners-in-captivity-and-brothers-in-arms-but-beyond-that-love-story—to have a fair crack at the audience prize too. It has to be thoroughly Rumantsch.

'What if we shoot it in Rumantsch?'

'That would go a long way to getting the Rumantschness of it, yes.'

'But?...'

'But it would obviously entail you having at least a working knowledge of Rumantsch.'

The prospect seems daunting, but I speak fairly decent Italian, workalike French and a little Portuguese. I once studied Putonghua for a while. And, it occurs to me now, a little Latin, back at school, which I didn't enjoy then, but that's a long time ago, and I didn't particularly see eye to eye with my teacher, except when we both agreed I should probably cease coming to his Latin class...

'I think the film needs to be trilingual,' Edgar offers into the silence that has briefly settled over my brow as I am contemplating my linguistic predisposition towards learning Rumantsch (I tried Spanish once too, but that didn't get me very far: the Italian kept interfering).

'What, Italian, French and Portuguese?'

'No, of course not: English, Swiss German and Rumantsch.'

'Why would anybody in this story speak English?'

'Because it's an English researcher or journalist or distant relative who happens upon it and tells it, from his perspective, today.'

'Like a meta-story.'

'A bit like a meta-story.'

'It's been done before.'

'Everything has been done before.'

'It's probably less of a meta-story, this, than a straightforward framework device.'

'It could work: you can write the English and the Swiss German dialogue, and I can translate the Rumantsch bits.'

'Is your Rumantsch good enough for that?'

'It will be by the time you're done with your script.'

'But you're not a writer.'

'No, you are.'

That's true. I am. It's a fascinating idea.
I could write the script in English and
Swiss German, and he could translate the
parts of the dialogue that need to be in
Rumantsch into Rumantsch, and then we'd
obviously need somebody whose mother
tongue is Rumantsch to check it for its
overall Rumantschness, maybe one of the
descendants: one of the clan.

I am beginning to imagine the kind of
conversation I would be having with an
alp farmer descendant of a Helvetian 17th
century mercenary who goes to rescue his
brother from captivity in a foreign land,
only to find that his brother doesn't really
want to leave because he doesn't want to
abandon his lover, because he is concerned
for his safety, and fears, quite reasonably,
that he will never see him again if he now
joins his brother and escapes back to his

village high up in the mountains, across the St Gotthard Pass. It sounds like an intriguing story to me. Has it got legs, though?

I think I'd need to sleep on it. At the moment, that's problematical...

Several weeks pass, during which I do my utmost to get at the Rumantschness of it all. This involves me using a long planned trip to Switzerland to traipse up into the Rumantsch-speaking part of the mountains and listen to their glorious choirs singing in small but packed churches, talking to native Rumantsch speakers (in Swiss German) about Rumantsch as a language, about their roughly half dozen dialects or 'idioms' (some of which don't even understand each other), and about Rumantsch culture.

I find out that there is really not so much of a Rumantsch tradition as there are small local traditions that fall under the Rumantsch umbrella, but much as with Swiss German, which has many more dialects, some of which also find it difficult to understand each other, many people identify much more with their regional dialect than with the language overall.

The Rumantsch dialects take their names from the valleys where they are spoken, or from the nicknames their speakers were given by their neighbouring valley dwellers, and to me they sound like poetry, like characters in a mythical story about great heroes, fabulous creatures, and the eternal melancholy of the mountains: Sursilvan, Vallader, Putèr: the people who live above the forest, the people from the valley, the porridge eaters; Surmiran, Jauer, Tuatschin...

Everything about the life of the people I thus encounter is so different to my life, everything about their history so remote from my history, that I might as well have landed myself in a different world, on

a different planet, but I am fascinated,
intrigued. Humbled, fairly, too, to think
what harshness, what overpowering awe
they have, over generations, had, and learnt,
to contend with, from these alps, from this
seclusion, from this climate: they can be
extreme.

I don't speak to or otherwise communicate
with Edgar for much of this time, seeing
that he is generally busy, at least as busy as I
am; and going by the convenient adage that
'no news is good news,' I assume him to be
well; and I feel content, immersed in my
new 'project'. It isn't so much a project as
the pursuit of a trail that I happened upon
(was really pointed towards, by Edgar),
following it now out of sheer curiosity
and that ever persistent Lure of the Alien.
That which is different. The other, the new.
It is not new to any of these people that
I meet with and ask for accounts of their

families' histories, and they look at me with a mixture of indulgence and bemusement, but I mind it not. They are wondrous to me, even exotic. They are not exotic to themselves.

Enriched with audio recordings, video clips, and a raft of pictures of possible locations and all manner of Rumantsch paraphernalia, I return to London to start drafting my treatment, and I forget, for another several weeks, completely Edgar's condition.

At the same time, I fall back into my own nocturnal pattern, staying up usually until three, four in the morning, or until my eyelids droop and I fall asleep, either having made it to bed around then, or occasionally also on the sofa, having watched *Newsnight* and intended to hang about quite a bit longer, or—this is quite rare—actually hunched over my laptop and realising I really have to get some sleep now. The worry about worrying about Edgar thus dispersed, I also don't worry about insomnia, and so, quite naturally, my own brief flirtation with what to me had always seemed at worst a relatively minor inconvenience appears to have ended. I remind myself that to people with insomnia it is anything but a minor inconvenience, and I wonder have I been selfish, so I decide to check on Edgar:

'How are you doing?'

'I'm doing fine, thanks, and you? Making progress?

'Of sorts. I should have a first draft in a couple of months or so.'

'I look forward to reading it.'

'What are you reading right now?'

'I've been reading Chaucer and rereading Pico della Mirandola.'

'Amazing.'

'They are.'

'You should read Shakespeare's sonnets.'

'I have.'

'You could read them again. – Are you sleeping?'

'Not much. Are you?'

'Back to normal.'

'Were you not sleeping normally before?'

'I'd been worried.'

'About what?'

'You, mostly.'

'Aw. That's sweet, but unnecessary.'

'I know.'

'And why did you stop worrying?'

'I got absorbed in the Rumantsch thing.'

'That's good.'

'I know.'

'Are you getting at the Rumantschness of it all?'

'I think so: I've been talking to dozens of people, including the descendants of the man who wrote the story about the brothers. They've been helpful.'

'Do they mind you plundering their family annals?'

'No, they seem a bit puzzled by my fascination with them. But they're forthcoming, of sorts.'

'That's good.'

'I know.'

I'm about to hang up, when it strikes me:

'Have you ever considered doing some research into why it is that people cannot sleep?'

'Not really, no.'

'Perhaps you should.'

'Why?'

'Well, perhaps if you understood the reasons why people have insomnia, then you could mitigate against suffering from it yourself.'

'I don't suffer that much, I'm taking melatonin.'

'Melatonin?'

'The sleep hormone.'

'You're taking hormones.'

'Temporarily.'

'I hope temporarily. – You shouldn't be taking them regularly over the long term.'

'Why not?'

'Because they might do damage. Most drugs do.'

'It's not a drug, it's a hormone.'

'Well quite: it might unbalance your hormone household.'

'It might?'

'I'm no expert.'

'Neither am I.'

'You could read up on it: you're an expert on most things.'

'I have recently become an expert at Go.

'Go?'

'Yes, the game.'

'That's quite difficult to get expert at, isn't it.'

'It is. Oh and Peruvian llamas. They're really quite whack. Did you know people use llamas to guard other animals, like sheep, for example?'

'I did not.'

'It's fascinating: though it's best to use a female llama or one single gelded male, apparently. If you use two or several gelded males they tend to hang out with each other and ignore their charges.'

'Haha, that makes sense.'

'And I know an awful lot about bamboo too, just in case you wondered.'

I hadn't really wondered about anything near as specific as that, but I'm glad to hear that Edgar's palette of expertise keeps growing, randomly, it appears.

Another two months or so go by quickly, and I hammer away at my treatment of the two mercenary brothers until I have got it in some sort of shape that I feel surprisingly happy with, and I give it another couple of days and read it through once or twice more and tweak it, and I reckon that's it, that's my Draft One Point Two (you never send out a Draft One Point One, to anybody; most people would advise you never to send out a Draft One at all), and I pick up the phone and call Edgar. He doesn't answer, it goes to voicemail. He must be in the shower, I reckon, or be talking to someone in China, or cooking (though he's not a late eater, and it's just gone midnight here, so it will be just gone one in the morning there), or working out a problem that interests him; he'll call me back shortly, I reckon.

He doesn't. I wonder what might have happened to him, but before I can really worry—and having rather resolved not to worry about Edgar again, because it's so patently unnecessary—I go back to work and do some more fiddling, until I doze off and briefly wake up again and decide it's time to go to bed; and I go to bed and fall asleep. Edgar calls me at ten in the morning, bright and breezy:

  'Edgar! How are you?'
  'Magnificent. How are you?
  'I'm well. You had me worried last night.'
  'Why?'
  'I thought you had fallen asleep or something.'

It's my feeble attempt at a joke. It fails:

'I had.'

'You had?'

'Yes! Thanks to you!'

'You're welcome. What happened?'

'Well I thought I should probably wean myself off the melatonin and allow my body to produce it itself in the required quantities at the appropriate times...'

'Quite.'

'...and so I stopped taking it.'

'And that solved your insomnia.'

'Of course not. It made it worse.'

'Oh dear.'

'Then I thought maybe you're right, maybe I need to become an expert on this, so I can treat myself more effectively in the long term.'

'Oh amazing: you're now an expert on insomnia!'

'I am nothing of the sort.'

'Ah.'

'I started doing some research, at a basic, you know, Wikipedia level, and it sets out really quite interesting.'

'I imagine.'

'But then you realise that there are a million possible reasons and as many possible interventions, and so there's zero scientific consensus except some pretty obvious observations about common sense behaviours and unending lists of things that may or may not be the case; and before I knew it I got so bored reading about it, I fell asleep.'

'Result.'

'Well yes. And the best thing about it: it's repeatable. Like you with your *Hitchhiker's Guide to the Galaxy.* It works every time, it's amazing. In fact, it works better now and faster, than it did three weeks ago, when I first discovered it: I now practically just have to google 'insomnia' and I start to feel drowsy, it's almost Pavlovian.'

'Congratulations.'

'Thanks! – So, what's new?'

'Oh: the treatment.'

'Ah yes?'

'I think I've cracked it.'

'You have?'

'Well I think I'm close: I've got a draft.'

'Cool. Send it over.'

'I will.'

And I do. And I'm wondering what he'll make of it, what will come of it, what to do with it, where to send it next, who to pitch it to, how to proceed, with what chance of success, if any; what's 'success' in this context, anyway; perhaps I went about it all the wrong way, this may have to be much more dramatic. Or funnier. Or tighter, I tend

to lose myself in tangents, sometimes,
but I didn't really in this case; maybe it
needs to be looser; perhaps it needs to be
more broadly relevant; more culturally
representative, more authentic, surely;
surely that: way more authentic, wittier,
warmer, dryer and softer. Sharper, more
humane—is it really the brothers' story
that matters? Could it not much more
be the mother's?—more diverse, more
character-driven, with a more female
perspective, more up-to-date, more
historically accurate, and altogether much
more Rumantsch.

And so yes, here I am, lying awake
through the night, wondering about the
Rumantschness of it all, with a picture in
my mind of a posse of guardian llamas,
chilling in the grass, chewing the cud, an
air of sophistication about their general
nonchalance, and the flock or the herd

or the peep they're supposed to look after
just nowhere to be seen...